Hudson's First Airplane Flight

VISITING GRANDPARENTS ON SUMMER BREAK

Author: Jagdish S Thakur
Illustrations: American Book Publisher

DEDICATION

TO MY PARENTS

Chapter 1:
Hudson and His Family

In a busy city, there lives a boy named Hudson. He lives in a cozy home with his little sister, Sydney, and his loving and caring parents. Hudson is a very active and playful boy. He enjoys reading storybooks and solving challenging puzzles. Hudson and Sydney often go for ice skating sessions or swimming after school with their mom and dad.

hool
BAKER'S
Bank

Chapter 2:
From Morning Plans to Evening Stories: Hudson's Routine

Every morning, Hudson eagerly talks with his mom about his plans for the day. He checks his toys to make sure nothing is missing and spends some time working on the unfinished LEGO mega city.

Chapter 2 (continued)

Hudson and Sydney enjoy visiting the park with Dad to explore birds, waterfalls, gardens, and sports courts. Whenever Hudson finds a blossoming plant in the park, he never forgets to bring a flower home for his mom.

Chapter 2 (continued)

In the evening, Hudson and Sydney help set the table for dinner. They love sharing stories from school while enjoying their mom's delicious cooking. Hudson and Sydney are always excited to chat with their grandparents on FaceTime and look forward to visiting them. Before sleeping, they love listening to magical stories while cuddling with their favorite stuffed animals.

Chapter 3:
A Mysterious Flying Object:
An Airplane

Since Hudson was a toddler, he has been fascinated by birds and often ran after them. It has always been a mystery to him how they can fly into the skies and go wherever they wish.

One day, while playing outside, Hudson saw something big and noisy flying overhead. He turned to his dad and asked, "What is it, Dad?" With a smile, his dad replied, "It's an airplane." Confused, Hudson asked, "Is it a kind of bird, and why is it making so much noise? Is she angry?"

Dad patiently explained, "No, son, it's not a bird, but it surely looks and flies like one. The noise is the sound of its engines. It's carrying many people, including children, in its belly and taking them to another town." Hudson became very fascinated with the mysterious flying object that carries people in its belly.

Chapter 4
A Sweet Surprise by Parents:
A Trip by Airplane

Hudson excitedly told his sister about the mysterious flying object, and she was equally surprised to learn about it. They both wondered if they would ever come close and touch it. Noticing the kids' strong curiosity about the airplane, Mom and Dad decided to surprise them.

A week before summer break at school, Hudson's parents had a big surprise for their kids. "Guess what, Hudson and Sydney?" Dad said with a smile. Hudson quickly asked, "What is it, Dad?" "We're going on an airplane trip!" Dad exclaimed. Hudson and Sydney were thrilled to hear this news. They had wanted to see an airplane up close and go inside its belly.

Chapter 5:
Hudson Gets Curious About the Trip

Hudson was curious and asked, "Where are we going, Dad?"

With a gentle smile, Dad replied, "We will visit your grandparents." Since Hudson will be traveling for the first time by airplane, Dad explained the difference between car and airplane travel: "Traveling by airplane is very different than traveling by car. For longer distances, traveling by airplane is faster and generally safer. Airplane travel follows schedules set by the airlines. While on your car trip, you choose your route, schedule, and stop whenever you wish.

When we take an airplane trip, we sit inside the airplane, which lifts us from the ground and takes us high up in the sky above the clouds. When you are up there, you will see a world that is so different from what you have seen before. So be ready for that."

Chapter 6:
Preparing for the Airplane Trip

Hudson and Sydney started thinking about their airplane trip and started packing their suitcases. Hudson chose his favorite bedtime books, a variety of puzzles, and his favorite stuffed dog, Bluey.

Meanwhile, Sydney excitedly gathered her favorite Barbie dolls and a selection of cozy pajamas for the journey ahead.

Mom and Dad also became busy packing their suitcases, ensuring they had everything they needed for their journey, and staying at their parents' home. With their suitcases filled with favorite items, Hudson and Sydney were wondering where they would take the airplane for their trip to their grandparents.

Chapter 7:
Driving to the Airport

Mom gathered the kids and explained that the airplanes are found at a special place called the AIRPORT. It's a home for airplanes where one can see hundreds of airplanes of different sizes.

On the day of their flight, Dad started loading suitcases and bags into the car. After breakfast, they began their drive to the airport, which was located on the other end of the city. For Hudson and Sydney, the dream of flying was becoming a reality as they got closer to the airport.

As they came closer to the airport, Hudson saw the airplanes flying above. "Look, Sydney, they're so huge!" he exclaimed. From a closer look, Hudson and Sydney became convinced that airplanes are very different from birds; they don't flap their wings, don't have feathers, and are huge and make loud noises, unlike birds. This was the first time they had seen such a big moving machine, and they were amazed to see it. Now, they are even more curious about going inside the airplane.

Chapter 8: Security Check-in at the Airport

After arriving at the airport, Dad informed everyone about the airplane travel rule: before entering the airport, we needed to go through security. Hudson and his family waited in a long line for the security check.

When they finally reached the security window, the officer, dressed in a blue uniform with a shiny metal badge, greeted Hudson and Sydney with a friendly smile. Dad handed over Hudson and Sydney's ID cards to the officer, who made sure that we were the same people who were on the ID cards. She looked at Hudson and asked if he was excited about his first airplane trip. "Yes!" Hudson replied. Sydney was also happy to meet the security officer. They thanked the security officer and moved on to the next step of the security check-in, which is body scanning.

PASSPORT

Chapter 9:
Navigating the Airport

After passing through the security check-in, Hudson, his little sister, Sydney, and his parents collected their suitcases, put on their shoes, and walked to the departure gate. This was a long walk inside the airport through a moving crowd and must be done carefully without making any mistakes. On the way, they were amazed to see hundreds of people of all ages eagerly walking in the hallway toward their departure gates. The family followed the overhead signs and headed to the departure gate through the busy crowd. Mom held Hudson's hand securely while Dad held Sydney's hand, making sure the whole family stayed together.

As they walked through the busy corridors, Hudson and his family passed numerous shops, food courts, and restaurants. Passengers stopped at the shops for a quick snack or last-minute souvenir. Hudson and Sydney were fascinated by the variety of chocolate and toy shops.

RESTAURANT
SOUVENIRES & GIFTS
SOUVENIRES & GI

Chapter 10:
Spotting Pilots and Flight Attendants

On their way to the departure gate, they saw a group of smartly dressed people rolling their suitcases along. Dad explained that some of them were pilots who fly airplanes, while the others, in uniform, were flight attendants. The flight attendants warmly greet everyone, hand out snacks and drinks, and help with anything needed during the flight. After a long walk, they reached their departure gate. Hudson and Sydney were filled with joy and excitement as they waited to board the airplane.

Chapter 11:
Welcome Aboard:
Entering the Airplane's Belly

After waiting for a while, it was announced that the passengers could start boarding the airplane. The check-in officer scanned Hudson and his family's boarding passes, and after that, they started walking down the long hallway toward the entrance to the airplane's belly. They slowly stepped on board. A friendly flight attendant greeted them with a big smile and said, "Welcome aboard." Hudson and Sydney boarded the airplane. On the left, at the entrance, they saw the pilots preparing for the flight. As they came inside the airplane, they saw people putting their suitcases in the overhead space and settling in their seats. Hudson whispered in Sydney's ear, "We are inside the belly of the airplane; it's amazing!" Sydney was also surprised and said in a low voice, "It's huge!" Hudson and his family started walking down the aisle, looking for their seat numbers.

Chapter 12:
The View from the Airplane Window

Hudson and Sydney settled into their seats and securely fastened their seat belts. Looking out the window, they saw many airplanes with colorful logos on their tails, some moving along the runway, others ready to take off. They were surprised to see the size of the airplane's wings. As they waited for the plane to take off, they attentively read the safety rules that the flight attendant was announcing. They learned about exit doors, life vests, flotation devices, and emergency oxygen masks. This experience introduced them to important information about air travel safety.

Chapter 13:
We're Flying Like Birds

After a while, the pilot announced that the airplane was ready to go. Slowly, it started moving toward the runway. "We're moving!" Hudson and Sydney exclaimed. The airplane came onto the runway, stopped for a moment, and then, with a loud noise, it started racing down the runway.

Outside the window, the world began to move faster and faster, and suddenly, the airplane lifted above the ground. "We're flying!" Sydney screamed with delight. They watched in wonder as the airplane went up and up, and the world below became smaller and smaller. As the airplane climbed higher and higher, Hudson and Sydney felt a sense of joy they had never experienced before and imagined that this must be how the birds felt when they flew.

Chapter 14:
Flying Through the Clouds

As the airplane continued flying higher and higher, it entered the fluffy white clouds with a small shaking in the airplane. "Look, Sydney! We're flying through the clouds!" Hudson exclaimed with wonder. Together, they watched the clouds pass by the airplane's wing. As the airplane continued going up, finally, it came out of the clouds. Hudson and Sydney were amazed to see a new world of blue sky, bright sun, and the ocean of clouds below. Hudson told Sydney, "It's a different world as Dad had described. There is nothing up here; it's empty as far as we can see; we don't see any birds flying up here." They were filled with joy as they continued their journey through this charming world up the clouds. Mom whispered to the kids, "Be ready for a picnic party; it's coming soon." Hudson and Sydney became very excited about the upcoming surprise.

Chapter 15:
Picnic Party in the Sky

After flying for some time, a friendly flight attendant came down the aisle with a cart, offering delicious treats to the passengers. Hudson and Sydney were excited and curious about the food items on the cart. "What would you like?" the flight attendant asked with a warm smile. Hudson chose a pack of cookies and orange juice, while Sydney said, "I want pretzels and apple juice." After thanking the flight attendant, they eagerly tore open their snacks and felt like they were having a picnic party in the sky. Although the snack time on the flight was a delightful moment of their journey, they were looking forward to meeting their grandparents.

Chapter 16:
Landing at Grandparents' City

After a while, the pilot announced that we were close to our destination. He started lowering the airplane's height. As the airplane started coming down, Hudson and Sydney felt a slight pop in their ears. They noticed the world below becoming bigger again. Finally, with a soft thud, the airplane touched the runway. It was still running very fast but gradually slowing down. Hudson and Sydney exchanged excited glances at each other.

As the airplane stopped at the terminal, the door was opened for the passengers to leave. Hudson and his family gathered their suitcases and left the plane. As they came out of the airport building, their grandparents were waiting with huge smiles and open arms. "Welcome, my darlings, Sydney, Hudson!" they exclaimed, giving Hudson and Sydney big affectionate hugs.

Grandpa started driving home. On the way, Hudson and Sydney eagerly shared their flight experience with their grandparents, who were very happy to hear their stories. They were looking forward to reaching the grandparents' house and refreshing the sweet memories of their last year's stay.

ARRIVALS
TAXI
TAXI

Chapter 17:
Grandparents' House:
A Perfect Place for Summer Break

After driving for a while, Hudson and Sydney reached their grandparents' house, which was the perfect place for their summer vacation. The grandparents' house always fascinated them; it had a vast collection of exciting and very old items, including metal toy trucks, a variety of hand tools, fishing lures, guitars, tube radios, Barbie dolls, and a grandfather clock that played music every hour. They also saw photos of their great-grandparents on a family tree picture displayed in the living room. Kids were also amused to see an old picture of their dad when he was Hudson's age, and Hudson looked exactly like his dad in the picture!

Chapter 18:
Grandparent Bonding
and Making New Friends

Hudson and Sydney enjoyed spending time together, exploring new adventures inside and outside the house. Indoors, they loved playing board games, making imaginative creations from clay, and helping their grandparents with small household chores. Grandma often surprised the kids with delicious homemade treats, and with Grandpa, they had great fun playing puzzles and card games. In the outdoors, they enjoyed bike riding and exploring the neighborhood. They also made friends with other kids in the neighborhood and carried home the memorable moments of their friendships.

Chapter 19:
The Magical Backyard
at Grandparents' House

For Hudson and Sydney, the grandparents' backyard was a magical garden filled with colorful flowers, a bird feeder, outdoor sitting furniture, and different types of trees and bushes at the outer edges of the backyard. During the summer, everything was green and blossoming. On the tree's branches, birds had built beautiful nests using dry grass and sticks. Occasionally, the backyard could surprise you; last year, Hudson found a chick that had fallen from its nest, and it was making noise. He was surprised to see that they had no feathers when they were small. With the help of Grandpa and a ladder, they put the chick back in the nest. Squirrels enjoyed climbing trees, jumping across branches and were always busy looking for food. Occasionally, rabbits also hopped into the backyard and munched on fresh grass. All these things together created an enjoyable atmosphere filled with natural wonders.

Chapter 20:
Saying Goodbye to Grandparents

For Hudson and Sydney, the summer break went by quickly, and it was time to return home. Grandpa and Grandma felt sad as Hudson and Sydney packed their suitcases and started looking forward to their next trip. Grandpa drove Hudson and his family to the airport, and with tears in their eyes, they affectionately hugged each other and said goodbye. As they separated, Grandpa reminded Hudson and Sydney to call on FaceTime once they reached home.

DEPARTURES
TAXI

Chapter 21:
Nighttime Flight Back Home

Hudson and Sydney's return flight was at nighttime. As they entered the airport, they were delighted to see the twinkling lights of different colors glowing around the terminal. Since they already had flight boarding experience, they moved happily through the security check-in and walked through the airport hallways, following Mom and Dad toward their gate. The flight was on time, so they boarded the airplane, found their seats, and eagerly awaited takeoff. Soon, the airplane taxied down the runway, and then, with a roar, it lifted off the ground and flew into the night sky. As the airplane went up and up, the city and cars' twinkling lights slowly faded away on the ground.

Chapter 22:
Journey Back Home
Through Twinkling Stars

Looking out the window, Hudson and Sydney were surprised to see a big world of darkness they had never seen before. But, in the far distances of the darkness, they saw millions of twinkling stars as if inviting them. As Hudson and Sydney continued flying through the darkness, they felt they were visiting distant places among these stars.

After flying through the night sky for a while, they started feeling sleepy. They snuggled into their seats, Mom covered them with their blankets, and they were soon fast asleep. When they woke up, they were surprised that the airplane had landed, and Mom and Dad were picking up their suitcases. Hudson and Sydney completed their memorable airplane trip and drove home. This year's trip to their grandparents' house was filled with beautiful experiences they would fondly remember for many years.

So, the next time you look up at the big blue sky, remember, like Hudson and Sydney, you can fly into it. Who knows what wonders await you up there in the starry skies?